This book belongs to:

_____

_____

_____

First published 1999 by Walker Books Ltd
87 Vauxhall Walk, London SE11 5HJ

This edition published 2011

2 4 6 8 10 9 7 5 3 1

© 1999 Lucy Cousins
Lucy Cousins font © 1999 Lucy Cousins

"Maisy" Audio Visual Series produced by King Rollo Films for
Universal Pictures International Visual Programming

Maisy™. Maisy is a registered trademark of Walker Books Ltd, London.

The moral right of the author/illustrator has been asserted

Printed in China

British Library Cataloguing in Publication Data:
a catalogue record for this book is available from the British Library

ISBN 978-1-4063-3471-5

www.walker.co.uk
www.maisyfun.co.uk

Maisy Dresses Up

Lucy Cousins

WALKER BOOKS
AND SUBSIDIARIES
LONDON • BOSTON • SYDNEY • AUCKLAND

Maisy has an invitation to Tallulah's fancy dress party.

What can she
dress up as?

She looks in her
dressing up box.

She could be a pirate – but Charley is dressed up as a pirate.

She could be
a queen – but
Eddie is dressed
up as a king!

She could be a firefighter – but Cyril is dressed up as a firefighter!

Maisy has a good idea! She will make a special costume.

Everyone else is already at Tallulah's house.

Then the doorbell rings and in comes... a zebra!

Oh, it's Maisy!

Hello, everyone.
It's party time.

Read and enjoy the Maisy story books

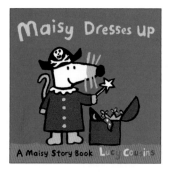

Maisy Dresses Up

A Maisy Story Book Lucy Cousins

Maisy's Bedtime

A Maisy Story Book Lucy Cousins

Maisy's Pool

A Maisy Story Book Lucy Cousins

Maisy Makes Lemonade

A Maisy Story Book Lucy Cousins

Maisy's Bus

A Maisy Story Book Lucy Cousins

Maisy Tidies Up

A Maisy Story Book Lucy Cousins

Maisy Makes Gingerbread

A Maisy Story Book Lucy Cousins

Maisy's Bathtime

A Maisy Story Book Lucy Cousins

My friend Maisy

Doctor Maisy

A Maisy Story Book Lucy Cousins

Maisy Goes Shopping

A Maisy Story Book Lucy Cousins

Available from all good booksellers

It's more fun with Maisy!